Greek Mythology

Gods and Folklore of Ancient Greece

Preface

Explore the fascinating world of Greek mythology through the folklore of ancient Greece.

Greek mythology is riddled with divine and mortal beings and their acts of bravery, fearsome disposition, and deeds that etched their name in the history of ancient Greece forever.

With riveting tales and a comprehensive introduction to all relevant actors in Greek mythology, this book will take you on an immersive journey through life in ancient Greece.

Table of Contents

Introduction

If there was ever a civilization that could give lessons about storytelling, it would be the ancient Greeks. The way they have woven their myths into their everyday life is truly fascinating, and that the tales were passed down through so many generations and survived until the modern age is even more riveting.

Due to the ancient Greeks' obsession with using mythology to record events and pass down the records over centuries of generation, books like this exist today. They can help you explore the ancient lore and all its actors, divine and mortal alike.

This book, in particular, is slightly different from the others on the market. Instead of just describing the Greek pantheon, it also explains its significance in ancient Greek life. Moreover, it also introduces you to the non-Olympian gods and goddesses, along with the heroes who performed great deeds without the advantage of divine powers.

For those interested in the creation aspect of Greek mythology, the book has a chapter dedicated to the way the ancient Greeks explained the formation of the world. As with all the other chapters, the information in this chapter is beginner-friendly and brings unique beliefs, thoughts, and ideologies to life.

The book also recounts the many ways the ancient Greeks incorporated religion into their daily lives to provide you with even more fascinating information about Greek mythology. After all, most of their myths and folklore had religious themes to try to explain otherwise incomprehensible situations and events.

Beyond reading well-known stories about the Greek gods and goddesses, you'll also learn how the Greeks believed these beings could interfere with their lives. You'll see religion intertwine with belief in nature and the efforts that were made to appease everyone who needed to be placated.

Learning about archaic civilizations is always rewarding. In many ways, their stories tell of their real lives, and this is no different for the ancient Greeks. As you'll learn, their relationships with their deities were much more than a fruitful source of stories. It was a way of life.

Whether you're well-versed in Greek mythology or it's your first time diving into this ancient world of wonders, you'll find something interesting and perhaps even surprising in this book. Prepare yourself for an in-depth exploration of mythological adventures — as well as a sneak peek of everyday life in ancient Greece.

If you're ready to begin this journey and sweep through a treasure trove of information, please, without further delay, start reading the first chapter. It begins with an easy-to-understand introduction of the Olympians, the Greek gods and goddesses you've likely heard of already.

Chapter 1

The Pantheon of Olympian Gods

Rising up high from the center of the Earth, Mount Olympus is the home of the Twelve Olympians. With its snow-peaked mountains and imposing presence, it was the perfect place for the ancient gods to dwell. They each have a palace, from where they command over their domains. The twelve deities all had distinct personalities, powers, and myths related to them.

This chapter will introduce you to these gods and goddesses, highlighting not only their domains but also their relationships, conflicts, and the story of how they conquered their predecessors, the Titans.

The Twelve Olympians

The Twelve Olympians were the most feared deities in ancient Greece, for they could inflict terrible punishments. However, they could also be kind and fair, which was another reason they played significant roles in the Greek worldview. They personified and ruled over aspects like seasons, wisdom, loyalty, music, and justice. Below is a more detailed description of these gods and goddesses.

1. Zeus

As the king of the Olympians, Zeus ruled over the entire Mount Olympus. His domains extended from natural aspects like lightning and thunder (or god of the sky, as he is referred to in some myths) to law and order. According to most myths, Zeus was a just and fair ruler, known to punish even gods if he felt they deserved it. For example, if someone broke an oath or lied, he would send a thunderbolt after them. Legend has it that he was gifted this thunderbolt by the Cyclops, whom he freed before defeating the Titans. Yet, Zeus was also a great peacemaker, often resolving conflicts between his siblings, other gods, and mortals.

2. Hera

Hera was the wife of Zeus and the queen of the gods and Mount Olympus. Representing the ideal woman, Hera was the proud patroness of marriage, family, and childbirth. However, she could be very possessive and jealous, especially when it came to her husband and children. In some myths, she was shown to be very vain and would retaliate for any slight against her.

3. Poseidon

The mercurial ruler of the seas, Poseidon, was almost as powerful as his brother Zeus. Despite his moniker, his domain included all bodies of water (i.e., oceans, seas, lakes, and rivers) and all the associated calamities. Greek mythology attributes natural disasters like hurricanes, earthquakes, and tsunamis to the wrath of Poseidon. He wasn't always destructive, for he was also the patron of horses, known to tame these animals with ease.

4. Athena

Athena was the divine ruler of wisdom, intelligence, knowledge, and reason. She was also the patron of craftsmen and could be called on for guidance in warfare. According to the stories, she was an excellent commander of strategic warfare and defense, probably due to her matter-of-fact and highly intelligent nature. She is often depicted in full armor, the same way myths claim she was born or, more precisely, emerged from her father, Zeus.

5. Ares

The fierce god of war, Ares, was the personification of masculinity and manly virtues. His name was tied to violence, battles, and bloodshed. According to mythology, Ares was known to ignite conflicts among gods and mortals, as he enjoyed seeing how events turned into a display of power. He was quick-tempered but was also noted for his courage and beauty.

6. Artemis

Just as passionate, Artemis, the goddess of the hunt, had a very widespread domain. Besides archery, hunting, and forests, she was also associated with protection, purity, virginity, and plagues. She was also the moon goddess who influenced nature through moon cycles and cleansing. Legend has it that Artemis asked for the gift of purity, hunting gear, and several nature spirits to help her oversee all nature when she was only three years old.

7. Apollo

Like his twin Artemis, Apollo was another complex ruler. His domain included the sun and light, medicine, plague, and healing. According to the myths,

Apollo taught people medicine and was the only god who couldn't lie. He was also the patron of poets and musicians. He served as an inspiration for many artists, often shown with a lyre. The sun is another of Apollo's symbols, in reference to his role as a sun god.

8. Aphrodite

The patron of beauty, passion, and fertility, Aphrodite was the Greek goddess of love. Known to incite desire and pleasure, Aphrodite contributed to procreation among humans. She was also involved in matters of commerce and warfare, often supporting one side with divine gifts. She was the patron of seafarers, along with courtesans.

9. Demeter

As another fertility goddess, Demeter had similar roles, except her domain was nature itself. She reigned over seasons and, according to the myths, helped humans have a productive and fruitful harvest season. She created fertile soils to ensure grains could be cultivated and fed to animals and is closely associated with agriculture.

10. Hermes

Often described as the trickster god, Hermes is the messenger of the Olympians. He delivered divine messages to people and was also associated with sleep. He was also the patron of trade and travel and could easily guide or hinder someone's voyage, depending on the mood he was in. He often pulled tricks on his siblings, even when he was a young child.

11. Hephaestus

Born with physical deformities, Hephaestus was an outsider among the Olympians; according to some myths, he was even cast out at one point. For people, however, he was the much-honored blacksmith god. Besides making all-powerful divine weapons and homes for the Olympians, he also taught people the art of weaponry. He was very clever, often ensnaring other gods in his traps and making deals for their release.

12. Dionysus

While generally known as the god of wine, Dionysus was truly associated with all kinds of alcoholic drinks, festivities, and even resurrection. According to some stories, the heavy drinking that drives people to madness is Dionysus' doing. Sometimes, he would act as a peacemaker between the other gods.

The Intricate Relationships of the Olympians

The Twelve Olympians all had some form of relationship with each other, and many of them were related as well. Due to this and living closely together, there were lots of conflicts, rivalries, and "bad blood" among them.

Zeus, for example, began his rule by overthrowing his father, Cronus. This was a mighty feat for the youngest son in the family. Then, he challenged his older brothers for a round of lot drawing over the rule. Having won the draw, he became the next ruler, which his brothers often resented. Zeus married his sister Hera, who was also a child of Cronus and Rhea.

While married to Hera, Zeus had many affairs, fueling Hera's jealousy even further. He fathered children with some of his mistresses. His daughter Athena was born out of his relationship with Oceanid Metis. Another daughter, Aphrodite, was the fruit of Zeus' affair with Oceanid Dione. With Leto, he had Artemis and Apollo, while with Maia, he fathered Hermes. According to one myth, Zeus once had a passionate love affair with Theban princess Semele, fathering the god Dionysus. Poseidon also had an affair with another one of his sisters, Demeter.

After losing the draw for the supreme rule, the other brothers had one draw to win the rule of the world. This is how Poseidon became the god of the sea and seamen. Poseidon married the beautiful Amphitrite, a descendant of the Titan Oceanus.

While married to Amphitrite, Poseidon also unsuccessfully courted his sister, the goddess Demeter. Not wanting to hurt Poseidon's feelings, Demeter dissuaded his efforts by finding a task for him. She asked Poseidon to create a beautiful animal. Poseidon began to make animals, but he was not pleased with any of them as he wanted to give the best gift to Demeter. He did it again and again until he was satisfied that he made the most beautiful animal, the horse. However, by the time he had finished creating the horse, he realized he wasn't even interested in Demeter anymore.

Due to his quarrelsome nature, Poseidon had many conflicts with other gods when he tried to overtake their cities. One of the most famous disputes is tied to the city of Athens, which was won by Athena, whom the city was ultimately named after.

Before becoming Zeus' wife, Hera was raised by Titans, Tethys and Ocean. At the beginning of their courtship, she wasn't interested in Zeus. Only after the god disguised himself as a cuckoo bird did he gain her sympathy. Once Hera took the bird into her arms, Zeus assumed his real form and took advantage of her, resulting in their marriage.

Hera was known to punish and torture her husband's mistresses and their children. She also participated in a revolt against her husband after the other gods grew dissatisfied with his overbearing rule. With Hera's help, the other gods drugged and tied Zeus, but he was subsequently freed by Briareus. Zeus punished Hera by hanging her from the skies overnight.

Ares was always seen as a coward and someone who could only resolve their issues by creating conflict. Due to this, he never had a good relationship with his siblings or even his parents, Zeus and Hera. He had an affair with Aphrodite, resulting in public humiliation from her husband, Hephaestus. By contrast, Athena was Zeus's golden child, the one who could do no wrong.

Due to his physical deformities, Hephaestus wasn't liked by his mother, Hera. Some stories say that Zeus wasn't his father, and when Zeus learned this, he pushed

Hephaestus off Mount Olympus. According to another myth, Hera was so upset about bearing an ugly child that she tossed him into the sea, breaking his legs and adding lameness to his other afflictions.

How the Olympians Became the Rulers of Mount Olympus

Before Zeus came to rule, the elder gods, the Titans, reigned over the world. According to a widespread mythical poem, Cronus, the leader of the Titans, received a prophecy that one of his sons would overthrow him. To prevent this, he swallowed all his sons as soon as they were born. When Zeus was born, his mother Rhea hid him from his father, giving Cronus a stone to swallow instead. Eventually, Cronus regurgitated the stone along with all the children he had swallowed. By this time, Zeus had grown up and began to assemble his siblings to fight against Cronus and the rest of the Titans. This epic battle, known as the Titanomachy, lasted 10 years. Then, Zeus called the lightning bolt-making Cyclopes and the rock-throwing Hecatoncheires to his aid, eventually defeating the Titans and trapping them in Tartarus.

Chapter 2

Lesser Deities and Divine Beings

Besides the Twelve Olympians, the Greek mythological landscape was punctuated by an assortment of lesser gods, divine beings, and spirits. This chapter will discuss these creatures, their roles in the world, and their influence on people's lives and environment.

The Titans

According to the ancient Greek creation myth, the first Titan, Gaea, emerged from Chaos, the vast void that existed before anything else in the universe. Gaea, the personification of Earth (also known as the earth goddess), created her realm and a son, Uranus, whom she married. Uranus became the god of the sky and fathered the rest of the elder Titans.

One of Uranus and Gaea's sons, Cronus, rebelled against his father and decided to overthrow him. Aided by his mother, Cronus castrated his father, ending his rule (some myths claim he died, others say he went into hiding in shame).

The rest of the Titans were also associated with planets and other natural phenomena. Cronus was married to Rhea, another powerful Titan and descendant of Gaea and Uranus.

Oceanus and his wife, Tethys, created and ruled over rivers, oceans, and the natural spirits inhabiting the waters. These included the three thousand ocean nymphs who could be found anywhere in these waters.

Hyperion, the ruler of light, was another imposing Titan. His domain included the moon, the sun, and dawn. He shared responsibility over the moon with another Titan, Phoebe, the mother of Leto, who would become the lover of Zeus.

The Titaness of justice and order, Themis, created her much-cherished children, the seasons, and the fates.

Mnemosyne, another Titaness, reigned over memory and was the mother of the Muses.

Other Titans mentioned in Greek myths are Crius, Thea, Iapetus, and Coeus.

Iapetus was the father of heroes like **Atlas, Prometheus, and Epimetheus.**

Coeus was one of the most intelligent Titans, almost as wise as Prometheus, and was known to foretell the future with uncanny accuracy.

Knowing the outcome of the battle between the Titans and Zeus' army, Prometheus chose to stand on Zeus' side.

In most myths, Prometheus was the protector of people, the role assigned to him by Zeus. In some stories, Prometheus also created mankind — with the help of his brother, Epimetheus. Prometheus taught people how to use fire and offer sacrifices from just the innards of animals, tricking Zeus into accepting these and letting people take the best part of the animals to feed their families. When Zeus learned this, he punished Prometheus by chaining him to a rock. Fearing he would succumb to the same fate as his father and grandfather, Zeus agreed to set Prometheus free if he told him whether one of his children would want to dethrone him. Before telling Zeus what he saw, Prometheus was freed by Hercules.

Unlike his brother, Epimetheus wasn't particularly bright. He was married to Pandora, the woman who unleashed all evil into the world.

Atlas, the third son of Iapetus, supported Cronus against Zeus. A few years into the battle, Cronus grew tired, and Atlas replaced him as the leader of the Titans in the battle. Like Cronus, he was also punished by Zeus and was condemned to hold the world on his shoulders.

Metis was the ruler of Mercury, a powerful Titaness who reigned over knowledge, communication, and wisdom. She was Zeus' lover and gave birth to their daughter Athena. According to some myths, Zeus received the prophecy that Athena would want to replace him, so he swallowed her. However, Athena lived on in her father's belly, empowering him with her endless wisdom. Her mother, Metis, died when Athena was born.

Other Olympian Deities

Hades

Hades, the ruler of the underworld and Zeus's brother was said to be just as powerful as the Twelve Olympians, but he wasn't included among them because he didn't live in Mount Olympus. He was highly respected and feared as the god of the underworld. He guarded the entrance of his realm, not allowing anyone to cross before their death. Only those who died could enter, the only exception being his wife Persephone, whom Hades brought to the underworld himself.

Persephone

Persephone was the daughter of Demeter, making her another powerful godess and the descendant of the Olympians. As the goddess of spring, Persephone was highly revered and worshiped by farmers before she entered the underworld.

As the story goes, as a young maiden, Persephone loved to play in the meadows. She would chase the nymphs among the flowers and laugh with joy. This is how Hades encountered her and was instantly captivated by her. He kidnapped her and was aided in this by Zeus. When Demeter learned that her daughter was missing, she went to look for her across the world, ultimately learning of Zeus' role in Persephone's abduction. Infuriated, she proclaimed that no fruit would mature on the Earth until her daughter was returned. Wanting to make peace, Zeus arranged for the girl's return, but it was too late. Persephone became Hades' bride and ate fruit from the underworld, which meant she had to stay there for at least part of the year. Ever since, she has lived in the underworld, returning only in spring, making meadows filled with flowers, and causing grains to grow in the fields. Before the onset of winter, she returns to the underworld, signaled by the death of greenery and the halting of growth of everything in nature.

According to other accounts, Persephone is only the goddess of the underworld, with her only responsibility being receiving those who freshly crossed the entrance. She guides them while they adjust to life in death, just as she has done with Orpheus and Herakles.

Hestia

Hestia was the oldest child of Cronus and Rhea, making her the sister of Hera, Zeus, Hades, Demeter, and Poseidon. As the first generation of deities, she was powerful but decided not to live on Mount Olympus. Some records list her as the Olympian goddess (as she has a palace at the home of the gods), while others say she resigned her residence forever because she grew tired of seeing her siblings bickering.

As the patron of fire, hearth, and family, Hestia had a gentle disposition and would rather create peace and harmony than punish or get into conflict with someone. In some accounts, she even peacefully gave over her home in Mount Olympus to Dionysus when the other deity wanted it.

Nature Spirits — Nymphs, Satyrs, and Others

Living in harmony with nature, other beings were also interacting with people and the higher gods. Two major groups were the nymphs and the satyrs, the nature spirits with different roles in the natural world.

Nymphs

Nymphs were beautiful, feminine creatures, often depicted surrounded by flowers. They were minor goddesses and the spirits of the natural world, ruling over everything from mountains and forests through seas and rivers to meadows.

Nymphs guarded natural beauties, overseeing their birth, growth, death, and renewal. They created flowers, greenery, and trees and nurtured wild animals. They also made wetlands, brooks, springs, and grottoes, their favorite hiding places.

Nymphs interacted with and aided the work of higher gods and goddesses. Mainades and Bakkhai nymphs were the companions of Dionysus. When she went hunting, the goddess Artemis was joined by huntress nymphs, while Poseidon had the Nereids nymphs as companions. The goddesses at Mount Olympus had handmaiden nymphs who acted as their servants. When he was sent to hide by his mother, Zeus was raised by Idaian nymphs.

Depending on where they lived, Nymphs were divided into fresh water, tree and forest, meadow and marsh, sky and star, sea, and underworld nymphs.

Oceanids (the innumerable daughters of the Titan Oceanus), Naiads, and Hydriads were freshwater nymphs. By providing water resources to the Earth, they nurtured the natural world. They lived along the springs, streams, rivers, fountains, and wells they created. They were also linked to rain clouds, flowers, and trees, which helped the water circulate between the Earth and the sky.

Dryads, Hamadryads, Meliae, Melissae, and Oreads were tree and forest nymphs. Dryads and Hamadryads presided over trees; the latter was always assigned a specific tree to oversee. Meliae and Melissae helped tree pollination by ruling over bees and were associated with mountain ash. The Oreads were mountain-dwelling creatures descending from the previous two groups.

Epimelids, Limonids, and Anthusae were meadow and marsh nymphs. The first two lived in and oversaw water meadows and pastureland, along with the animals grazing these. The third group was flower nymphs, responsible for the nurture and fertility of flowerbeds in meadows.

Nephelae, Aurae, Hesperids, and Asteriae were sky and star nymphs. Nephelae controlled rain clouds, Aurae brought cool breezes, Hesperids provided the beauty of sunset, and Asteriae brought out the sky. Other than Asteriae, who were daughters of Atlas, the rest of the sky and star nymphs were descendants of Oceanus, Boreas, and Hersperos.

Haliae were sea nymphs who ruled over waves, sandy beaches, coastal caverns and rocks, and fish. Nereids were also sea nymphs descending from Haliae.

Lampads were underworld nymphs guiding the arriving soul with their torches. They often accompanied Persephone and Hekate.

Other spirits in Greek mythology included the Maenads, who acted as companions to the gods and satyrs like the Silens.

Satyrs

Unlike the ethereal nymph, the satyrs were a bit more rustic, typically residing in the countryside and wild natural settings. They were shown to have man-like forms but also resemble animals, with their horse tails, dog noses, and donkey ears. The oldest also sported white beards and hair (or were bald with white beards), a big belly, and ox horns.

They ruled over fertility but had specific roles, depending on to which group of satyrs they belonged. For example, the Silens were the elders who oversaw the work of other satyrs and acted as companions to gods and the Titans beforehand. The elders were born from Seilenos, the wisest and oldest of the elder satyrs. They fathered other satyrs and a group of mountain nymphs called Oreiades.

From Gaea to Rhea to Hermes, Dionysus, and Hephaistos, many gods were known to interact and join forces with satyrs to help mankind or teach them a lesson. According to some accounts, the twelve guardians of Dionysus were also Silens.

Satyrs often accompanied Dionysus in his drinking escapades and were many times depicted dancing and playing amongst themselves or around the gods. These were called Tityroi, or flute-playing spirits. They also loved to play sports with the Mainades. There were also child satyrs, who were very playful and often played tricks on each other and people.

The Panes, a group of satyrs also called daemons, were goat-footed spirits wandering the highland pastures. They protected the animals grazing on these lands. They were also said to be very passionate supporters of fertility.

Chapter 3

Heroes and Mortals in Myth

Besides the gods, Greek mythology is also riddled with stories about divine heroes and mortals who showed extraordinary strength. Often finding themselves at the mercy of fate and prophecies, some are remembered for their courage, while others for their tragic destinies. This chapter will explore their myths, personalities, and other elements that played a significant role in their lives.

Famous Demigods and Heroes

As their name implies, demigods were half-gods, meaning only one of their parents was a deity. They were the children born from love affairs between gods and mortals. They often possessed special talents like the power to control the elements or superhuman strength. Below are the most famous demigods in Greek mythology.

Hercules

Hercules' unmatched strength came from his father, Zeus's, side. His mother was Alcmene, a mortal woman, one of Zeus' lovers. Countless stories describe Hercules' superhuman abilities, including the slaying of the Nemean Lion or the capture of Cerberus, the three-headed guardian dog of the gates of the underworld — feats of which no other mortal was capable.

Throughout his life, Hercules persevered through many trials, including a journey beyond the known world where he had to use his wits and all his might to perform impossible tasks. He was also frequently daunted and put to trial by Hera, whose jealous wrath often descended on Hercules as an illegitimate child of Zeus. According to one account, Hera made serpents appear in the infant Hercules' crib, but even at this tender age, Hercules was able to kill the venomous animals.

Later on, when Hercules married and had children, Hera inflicted rage upon him, causing him to slaughter his entire family. Devastated, Hercules turned to Eurystheus for help. Unfortunately, Eurystheus became another one of Hera's pawns against Hercules, sending Hercules on a journey full of grueling trials. Still, with unwavering determination, Hercules bravely fought through it all and, proving that strength comes from within, persevered against the odds.

Perseus

Perseus was another hero known for his extraordinary monster-slaying skills. He was born from the affair of Zeus and Danae, the mortal daughter of the king Acrisius. Perseus was surrounded by intrigue from the time he entered the world. A prophecy predicted that he would grow up to have incredible strength, which resulted in his exile from his home when he was still an infant.

Despite his less-than-fortunate start to life, Perseus did become a mighty hero, achieving feats like the defeat of Medusa, the sea monster who turned everyone who looked at her into stone. With his courage and strength preceding him, the gods gave Perseus several gifts to help him slay Medusa. Hades gave him a helm of invisibility, Athena gave him a reflective shield, and Hermes gave him winged sandals. When he encountered Medusa, Perseus had another challenge to overcome. Namely, Medusa held hostage Andromeda and was about to attack her. Thinking quickly, Perseus used the shield to reflect Medusa's gaze onto herself.

Protected by the shield, he quickly severed Medusa's head, saving Andromeda, who would later become his wife.

Another tale claims that Perseus used the head of Medusa to turn Polydectes, the king who attacked his mother, to stone. After doing this, Perseus handed over the head to Athena. These and similar stories show how Perseus overcame insurmountable challenges and became the brave and wise hero who established the city of Mycenae.

Achilles

Perhaps the best known hero of all time, Achilles, was the son of the sea nymph, Thetis, and the mortal king, Peleus. According to the popular narrative, fearing that her son would be defenseless against the divine beings, Thetis dipped him into the River Styx. Holding the infant by his legs, she forgot to submerge his heel, which became the only vulnerable point on his body.

Achilles grew up to become a fierce warrior with unmatched battle skills. In the Trojan War, his abilities became indispensable, ultimately leading to the slaying of Hector, a Trojan prince. However, amid the victories, his life was also punctuated by tragedies. He saw the death of his friend Patroclus, the event that ignited his wrath and led to his ultimate victory during the war. As illustrated in Homer's Iliad, Achilles was ultimately killed by an arrow to his heel — a deliberate shot from the god, Paris.

Achilles' stories show that as powerful, strong, and brave the demigods were, they were just as vulnerable. They couldn't escape their fates any more than mortals could.

Theseus

Theseus, the hero known for his bravery and intelligence, is of unclear origins. One narrative claims that he was the son of Aethra and Aegeus, both mortals. Other myths say that his father was the god Poseidon, which would make him a true demigod. Regardless of which narrative you follow, all depictions of Theseus' later life stand testimony to his extraordinary feats. One of them was slaying the Minotaur in the Labyrinth of Crete. According to the myths, Minos, the king of Crete, kept a Minotaur incarcerated in a labyrinth, feeding it humans. When he conquered Athens, Minos ordered a group of Athenians to be tossed into the labyrinth as a sacrifice to the Minotaur. Theseus was in this group, but Ariadne, Minos' daughter, fell in love with him and gave him a ball of red yarn so he could find his way out of the labyrinth. Theseus killed the Minotaur, and, with the help of Ariadne's yarn, he emerged from the cave alive and victorious.

After becoming their next king, Theseus helped the Athenians rebuild Athens into one of Greece's greatest cities. His rule was based on fairness and democracy, milestones that marked the coming civilizations.

Jason

Jason was the son of Acidente, the descendant of Poseidon, and Aeson, the king of Iolcos. He was also the descendant of Hermes, carrying plenty of divine essence in his blood. He used his skills and abilities to pursue adventures and noble goals, many of which led him against fearsome enemies like harpies and dragons.

Leading a band of heroes called Argonauts via Argo was probably Jason's biggest feat in Greek mythology. They were in search of the famous Golden Fleece, the prize Jason was to bring back to his uncle to reclaim his throne. Years before, Jason's uncle Pelias killed all Aeason's descendants so he could claim to be his brother's only heir. However, one of Aeson's sons, Jason, was saved and later returned to defeat Pelias. To obtain the Golden Fleece, Jason had to slay the dragon guarding it.

Unfortunately, Jason's trials continued even after he defeated his uncle. He was betrayed and lost his throne again. Through courage, perseverance, and the help of the friends he had made on his quests, he was able to reclaim it once again, leaving a legacy for his sons. He also went through tribulations in matters of the heart. Married to Medea, the sorceress granddaughter of Helios, Jason also had affairs, fathering several children with his lovers. When Medea learned of his betrayal, she killed several of his sons.

Atalanta

The daughter of Iasus and Clymene, the Orchomenian princess and descendant of Poseidon, Atalanta was the only female member of the Argonauts. She was a unique demigoddess who preferred hunting to feminine occupations. She was the protege of Artemis, the goddess of the hunt, who taught her how to use her superhuman speed.

Atalanta's determination to dominate in masculine occupations stems from her childhood. Her father, desiring a son, abandoned her in the forest, where she was found by a bear who took care of her during her infant years. Miraculously, she survived and was discovered by hunters who took her in.

Wanting to prove she could be just as strong, swift, and independent as any man, she entered the famous Calydonian Boar hunt. Instead of encouragement, she was surrounded by suitors who tried to persuade her to quit the race. Ultimately, she fell victim to the strongest power in the world: love. During a footrace amid the hunt, a fellow competitor, Hippomenes, fell in love with her. Knowing he couldn't beat her alone, he asked Aphrodite for help. The goddess gave him three golden apples, which he used cleverly as a distraction, winning the race and Atalanta's heart.

Odysseus

Odysseus, the victorious king of Greece in the Trojan War, was also known for his brave actions on his way home after the war. His return took him across a ten-year journey, during which he faced many calamities across the sea. He defeated the two Cyclops, Scylla and Charybdis, and had to withstand the deathly lure of sirens.

When he returned home, Odysseus learned that he was thought to be dead. Not wanting to reveal himself, he disguised himself as a beggar and began to court his wife, Penelope. However, he wasn't the only one, and ultimately, Penelope decided to challenge her suitors. She asked them to shoot an arrow through the heads of twelve axes, a feat none of them could do — except Odysseus. Proving that he was the most skilled and fearsome of all men, Odysseus finally revealed himself, killed the other suitors, and reclaimed his wife and kingdom.

Bellerophon

Bellerophon is another renowned Greek hero known for slaying the lion-headed monster Chimera. Before this feat, Bellerophon also captured Pegasus, the winged horse he used to defeat Chimera. Combining his own strength with the horse's swiftness, Bellerophon crept up on the monster and defeated it.

Unfortunately, the tale of Bellerophon is also one of caution, for he became overly confident in his abilities. After slaying Chimera, he began believing nothing could kill him, leading to his downfall.

Aeneas

As the son of Aphrodite, Aeneas was destined to be a hero. In addition to his strength, he was also gifted with visions and prophetic skills. This demigod was one of the Trojans' greatest leaders, triumphing in many battles against Greece. Even though the Greeks emerged victorious from the war, they couldn't defeat Aeneas. He would survive the last battle, along with Paris and Hector. According to one story, Aeneas was able to survive because he had a vision of Hector warning him and directing him to flee far away.

Orpheus

Orpheus is the proof of how diverse the landscape of Greek heroes was. Orpheus was a man whose only talent was tied to music and poetry. However, the story of how he used these to persevere against all odds is one of the greatest in Greek mythology.

When his wife Eurydice died from a snakebite, Orpheus was devastated. Seeing his suffering, the gods told Orpheus to go to the underworld and persuade Hades to let him retrieve his wife. Resistant at first, Hades' heart softened after hearing Orpheus' beautiful music. With the condition of walking ahead and never looking back until they reached the entrance of the underworld, Hades let Orpheus and Eurydice go. Unfortunately, Orpheus looked back at the last moment, losing his wife in an instant.

Oedipus

Oedipus, the hero whose life was just as tragic as it was heroic, is another honorable mention among the Greek heroes. According to the well-known narrative, a prophecy predicted that Oedipus would kill his father, King Laius, and marry his mother. To avoid this, Laius banished Oedipus, leaving him to die in the mountains.

After being raised into adulthood by King Polybus and Queen Merope, Oedipus learned about his prophecy from Pythia, the Oracle of Delphi. Believing Polybus and Merope to be his parents, Oedipus left their kingdom to avoid accidentally fulfilling the prophecy. On his way to another kingdom, he encountered and killed an old man. When he arrived at this kingdom, he learned that the king was dead, so he decided to ask for the queen's hand in marriage. The queen agreed, and they were married shortly after. It was years later when Oedipus learned that the old man he killed was the king and his own father to boot. He unwittingly fulfilled the prophecy he wanted to avoid.

The Relationship Between the Gods and the Mortals

The ancient Greeks strongly believed that the gods, goddesses, and other mythical creatures interfered with people's lives. Some did it to entertain themselves. Others did it out of affection. There are countless stories of the deities befriending or having a love affair with mortals. Athena, for example, was a supportive friend to Odysseus, constantly helping him out. Odysseus, in turn, greatly appreciated Athena's friendship.

Aphrodite also helped Troy in matters of love, albeit not for selfless reasons. According to the myths of Helen of Troy, Paris coveted Helen, the most beautiful woman he had ever seen. His efforts to make Helen his wife (even at the cost of deadly war) were aided by Aphrodite. However, the tale of the Judgment of Paris reveals another side of the story. Namely, Aphrodite used the promise of Helen as a bribe in a contest between her, Hera, and Athena. The three goddesses wanted a golden apple made by Eris. Under Zeus' command, Hermes told them to go to Paris and let him determine who should have the apple. Each offered the gift to Paris, Aphrodite's being offered to Helen. Paris decided that the apple should go to Aphrodite so he could have Helen as well.

Other gods strictly believed mortals should honor them and abide by their rules and the order they set in the world. If someone didn't follow these rules or did something wrong, they would be punished. The infamous son of the nymph Liriope and the river god Cephissus, Narcissus, experienced just how cruel the gods' punishment could be. Said to be extraordinarily beautiful, Narcissus made heads turn everywhere he went. Mortals and divine creatures had professed their love for him (including the Oread nymph Echo), but all in vain because he rejected them all. Seeing his disregard for others' affections, Nemesis, the goddess of retribution, decided to teach Narcissus a lesson. One day, following Nemesis' guidance, Narcissus stopped at a lake, where he saw his own reflection in the water and instantly fell in love with it. When he realized that he had fallen in love with himself and that his love would never be returned, Narcissus fell into despair and took his own life.

Chapter 4

Myths of Creation and the Cosmos

This chapter will offer insight into the Greek creation myths and views of the afterlife. Besides exploring topics such as the origins of the universe and all its inhabitants, the chapter will also tell the story of the Age of Men and all layers of the underworld.

The Ancient Greek Creation Myth

Like all cultures, the ancient Greeks had their own legends of how the world was created. While there are different renditions of the Greek Creation Myth, most agree that it all began with the actions of higher beings and then continued with the conflicts of these beings. Much like people, gods, and other mythical beings wouldn't always get along, causing all sorts of calamities during the creation of everything.

Chaos, the primordial void that existed in the beginning, might have been a god (or, more precisely, an embodiment of a god), although accounts of this vary.

What they all agree on is that when Chaos ruled, there was nothing but dark emptiness. There were no lands, water, sun, moon, mountains, or even air. There was no order, and the careless god (as Chaos is often described) preferred it this way.

Out of boredom, Chaos shaped darkness into the form of Nyx, a black bird with massive wings and the representation of Night in Greek mythology. Nyx then laid a golden egg and sat on it for a long time. Under Nyx's protection, life arose in the egg, and Eros was born. One half of the eggshell became Earth, later named Gaea, and the other became the sky or Uranus. Eros made the Earth and sky fall in love, creating a union that led to the creation of other beings.

In another version of the story, Nyx and Chaos made Erebus (Darkness) together, giving him the underworld. Erebus married Nyx and they had two children, Hemera (the embodiment of the day) and Aether (fresh air). The two children also mated with each other, and out of their union were born Gaia, Tartarus (the plane of the underworld equaling Hell), Eros (the god of love), and Pontus (the personification of the sea).

Nyx was a much-feared being, just like the massive force she created out of her children, all of whom represented a feared or detested aspect of life in Greek mythology. Among others, Nyx gave life to the Hesperides (the Daughters of the Evening), Moros (Fate), Momos (Blame), Ker (Doom), Philotes (Sexual Pleasure), Thanatos (Death), Apate (Deceit), Hypnos (Sleep), Eris (Strife), Oneiroi (Dreams), Nemesis (Revenge), Geras (Old Age), and Oizus (Pain).

As the descendants of Chaos, these four siblings played a crucial role in all versions of the later stage of the Greek Creation Myth. Gaea, for example, made a son, whom she married, and together, they had the twelve primordial Titans: Coeus, Crius, Hyperion, Lapetus, Oceanus, Cronus, Mnemosyne, Phoebe, Rhea, Tethys, Themis, and Theia.

Besides the Titans, Gaea and Uranus had other children, including three Hecatoncheires and three Cyclops. As their name implies, Hecatoncheires were giants with a hundred hands and almost as powerful as the Titans. Their names were Gyges, Cottus, and Briareus. The Cyclops were likewise gigantic but had only one eye in the middle of their foreheads. When they moved together, they created the noise of lightning and thunder. Named Steropes, Arges, and Brontes, these creatures were the first smiths who made weapons for the gods.

While prolific in creating them, Uranus didn't care much for his children. Titans, Cyclops, and Hecatoncheires were a nuisance to him, and he decided to hide them from their mother. Gaea wasn't happy with this, and she fully supported Cronus when he decided to rebel against his father. After ambushing and castrating Uranus with Gaea's sickle, Cronus threw his father's severed male parts into the sea, leaving a trail of blood behind them. According to a popular narrative, many beings were born from these drops of blood. Besides Aphrodite, who is said to emerge from the sea from the place Uranus' male part was dropped, Giants, Nymphs, Demigods and goddesses, and Erinyes (also known as Furies, the snake-haired women who enacted punishment ordered by Titans and gods) were created from Uranus blood.

The Cyclops and the Hecatoncheires remained trapped even after Cronus defeated Uranus but were later freed by Zeus, and, as a result, they helped him destroy Cronus and the Titans.

After overthrowing his father, Cronus married his sister, Rhea. He became the king of the gods and fathered gods and goddesses, some of whom would become members of the Twelve Olympians. These children, including Zeus, who eventually dethroned their father, would fight among themselves for a long time before finally agreeing to work in unity. Once they joined forces, they started adding more creations to the world. They put stars in the sky, placing them under the charge of Uranus. They also began to populate Gaea with life, adding more creatures and, eventually, animals and people to its landscape.

The Creation of Humanity and the Ages of Man

After all gods, nymphs, and other spirits were made, the Earth still lacked animals and humans. Zeus ordered his sons Prometheus and Epimetheus to remedy this by populating the Earth with animals and people and giving each a gift.

Prometheus then created people in the image of gods, and his brother formed the animals. Epimetheus finished his work much sooner than his brother and even handed the animals gifts when Prometheus finally completed making people. However, when he thought of what gift he could give to people, he struggled to find any because his brother had used all the gifts Zeus had ordered to be given out.

Thinking quickly, Prometheus gifted people fire. He brought some fire to them and told them how to use and create more. Humans began to thrive on this gift until another divine gift introduced everything evil to their lives. Zeus gave a beautiful woman, Pandora, to Epimetheus to marry. As a wedding gift, Zeus gave Pandora a box but prohibited her from ever opening it. Unable to withstand her curiosity, one day, Pandora opened the box, releasing all evil to the world. Epimetheus tried to remedy the damage by closing the box, but it was too late. The only thing left to do was to release the last item from the box, hope, so at least people could have hope when they had to face all the evil.

The Ages of Man

The story of the Five Ages of Man originates from the 8th century BCE. It was recorded by Hesiod, a shepherd and one of the earliest poets of ancient Greece. According to a myth, Hesiod was inspired to write the story after meeting the Nine Muses, the daughter of Mnemosyne and Zeus. He then proceeded to write several Greek mythology-themed poems, including the ones chronicling the lineage of mankind through five ages.

The Golden Age

In the mysterious Golden Age, the Earth was inhabited by the people who were created in honor of Cronus (or by him, depending on which storyline you follow). These people, while mortal, lived like deities without worry or trouble in their lives. They didn't have to work, they were always happy, and life was one perpetual spring for them. They died happy, too, mostly because they aged backward. When they died, they looked like children who had fallen asleep. In the afterlife, they became daemons who wandered the Earth. This age, full of radiance, blessedness, and all the best (hence the name Golden), ended when Zeus and his brothers defeated the Titans.

The Silver Age

During the Silver Age, people were under the rule of Zeus and made to look vastly inferior to the Olympians. They had to work and seek shelter to survive. They also had four seasons, which they had to use wisely by growing produce to feed themselves throughout the entire year. Fortunately, they still had their longitude, as children could live up to 100 years before they became adults. When they died, Silver Age people lived as blessed spirits in the underworld. On the flip side, they never learned about the concept of god worship, which infuriated Zeus. Deciding that people should honor him, Zeus destroyed the man of this age and went on to create new ones.

The Bronze Age

Made from the tough wood of the ash tree, the Bronze Age people were hardened warriors. They hunted and lived on meat, leaving the grain-made bread behind. Their homes, just like their armor, were made of bronze (bronze in ancient Greece was often associated with weaponry). When they died, they went to the underworld, where they lived according to the lives they had led and the acts they had accomplished while walking the Earth. The Bronze Age ended when people were destroyed by the flood which occurred during the life of Deucalion and his wife, Pyrrha, who created a generation of humans after the flood.

The Age of Heroes

Populated by the men and women created by Deucalion and Pyrrha, the Age of Heroes is also commemorated in Homer's work. During this period, people commingled and interacted with gods and demigods, many of whom became great heroes. Due to the interference of gods, demigods, and spirits, this was a fairer time for people. Still, many heroes met a tragic fate, whether due to betrayal from their closest ones or by being killed in one of the many Greek wars. After death, people of this age went to the underworld, or if they were very particularly heroic, received eternal bliss on the Island of the Blessed.

The Iron Age

The Iron Age was Hesiod's period and denotes the time when people had already encountered evil, which made many of them selfish or sorrowful. Completing the timeline from primitive innocence to evil, this age saw people becoming burdened with worries and losing virtues. They also lost the gods' support, for all deities stopped visiting the Earth and interacting with people. It was a troublesome time (it is named after a hard-to-work-with metal, after all), which Hesiod predicted would end with Zeus destroying people once again.

The Greeks View on the Afterlife

The ancient Greeks believed that people lived on after death. They crossed to the underworld, which had multiple layers, with unimaginable torture awaiting the sinners. Often described as a dark, shadowy place, the underworld consisted of the Plains of Asphodel, Elysium, and Tartarus. The latter was the darkest pit of the underworld, reserved for those who deserved punishment (for example, Zeus banished the Titans to Tartarus). After receiving their penalty, many of them were forgotten, left to wander perpetually in Tartarus.

Elysium was the new home of warriors who died in heroic deaths and were remembered for their courage on the battlefield. Living on in Asphodel was the reward of mortals who lived righteous lives and were remembered as loving and kind people by the living.

The river Styx, named after its patron goddess, lies close to the entrance of the underworld. Its ruler, Styx, the daughter of Titans Thetys and Oceanus, also resided in Hades' realm. Those who entered the underworld had to cross the river before moving on to their final home in the afterlife.

Besides Hades, Styx also allied herself with Zeus and sided with him against the Titans. For this, Zeus rewarded her with a great honor, using her water during the oath ceremony for the gods. Any god who broke their oath made on the water of Styx had a terrible punishment to look forward to.

Some, for example, mortal heroes descending from the Olympians, may have been granted eternal paradise, but most people had a murky existence after death. This didn't stop people from striving to ensure a blessed afterlife while still living. They held festivities, which promised a good life in the world of the living and the underworld. According to some narratives, being devoted to Dionysus or Orpheus could also provide mortals with the prospect of a better life after death. Rituals for small groups were performed, offering transformational experiences that people couldn't gain by simply leading a virtuous life and attending public religious ceremonies.

Regardless of where they ended up, the dead were under the rule of Hades, the god of the underworld, and his wife, Persephone. It was believed that honoring these deities would improve the lot of those who ended up in their realm. Coupled with virtuous behavior and worship rituals for other deities, avoiding Hades' wrath was another priority. He had the power to delegate the souls to any plain of the underworld and to deny assistance to those who freshly crossed its entrance.

Exploring the myths related to creation and the afterlife can provide a foundation for understanding how the ancient Greeks made sense of the universe and everyone's place within it. It is clear that this was a culture that relied on guidance and reverence of their deities, who had the power to create or destroy anything on a whim if they chose to. Their power extended from this world to beyond, and a person's fate in this life and the afterlife depended on their relationship with the gods.

Chapter 5

Folklore, Rituals, and Worship

Like the mythology of every other culture, Greek myths were born to explain meaningful and otherwise inexplicable occurrences in the world. They all had lessons, whether religious or personal. They taught people about puzzling events no one understood, but when connected to the acts and nature of gods, they all made sense.

For these reasons, religions and mythology were deeply interwoven into the fabric of life in ancient Greece. Myths were passed down through folklore, and the actors of these tales were honored through worship and rituals. This chapter will show how ancient lore combined with the polytheistic religion influenced everyday activities and how acts like sacrifice and oracles worked in ancient Greece.

Mythology and Everyday Life in Ancient Greece

In ancient Greece, mythology and religion went hand in hand. Not only were regular and public religious manifestations popular, but the Greeks also made sure that they would honor the mighty and sometimes feared gods and goddesses in everyday life. Do otherwise, and you might as well be denying the existence of these divine beings — and suffer the consequences. The Greeks believed that most gods (especially Zeus and the other Olympians) would not tolerate disobedience or any neglect to honor them regularly.

The religious manifestations weren't always confined to temples. They were also present in homes, public gatherings, sports competitions, and even arts and crafts. All of these had one thing in common: they were created or held in honor of the gods and goddesses present in the Greek mythological landscape. Everyday objects in works of art were often shown in mythological scenes, and many places and people were named after famous characters from mythology. Cities and people were also named after divine beings or heroes.

By giving a sacrifice, the Greeks believed to give up something of value, an act the gods would appreciate. Through sacrifice, they also showed the gods that they respected their authority. Most of the time, sacrifice included items of value like animals, which were considered highly precious for all the benefits (food, shelter, medicine, offering) they provided to people. They would likely offer a goat or a pig, making it into a feast for the deity in whose honor the sacrifice was made. After ceremoniously giving the animal to the deity, they would cook it over an open flame and offer the best pieces to the god. Then, whatever was left became a feast for the participants. Human sacrifices were rarer, but they also happened in ancient Greece, typically as a punishment or display of power over the just conquered enemy.

The religious rituals dedicated to deities in sanctuaries were held in the city that fell under the deity's patronage. Depending on which environment the deity preferred, the sanctuaries were either built out in an open field or in the city center. These sanctuaries were set aside from their environment with a large wall and often contained statues, an altar, and a place for making votive offerings. Sometimes, they also included springs or trees associated with the deity in whose honor they were built. Or, in the case of temples built in the name of Poseidon, they had a view of open water from at least two sides.

Sacrifices always took place in front of temples and sanctuaries, never inside them. This is because these sacred places were the home or the embodiment of the gods and goddesses. Most mortals couldn't enter, especially not during votive rituals. For most deities, there was an annual worship ceremony open to the public. Other ways to honor the gods included festivals like the four famous celebrations held at Nemea, Olympia, Delphi, and Isthmia, attended by people from all over Greece. They included ceremonies, rituals, athletic competitions, and processions, honoring the deities in every way possible.

Sacred Sites and Oracles

As beautiful as they were, ancient Greek temples were only to be admired from the outside. They were simple, but the interiors, where the essence of the gods or goddesses lived, held much significance. Most temples were built in an East-West direction because this was the best way to center the deities' essence in the natural world. Another reason for this was that many rituals were tied to the moon and/or sun, and this direction aligned perfectly with sunrise and the rhythms of the day and night.

Outside, worshipers were greeted with statutes, some of which had columns shaped into a woman-like form, especially if the site was dedicated to a female deity. Around the columns was the true worship place at every temple or sacred site. Here is where people could come to pray, consult the deity, or offer sacrifices to them. The priests may enter the temple itself but only once or twice a year. This was mainly to ensure everything was in order or, rarely, to convey a crucial message to the deity. Priests acted as divine messengers but usually received messages outside, in front of the other participants of a ceremony or ritual.

The Greek priests usually had many other jobs as well; they took on the extra duty of conveying messages or holding worship ceremonies because they believed this was a great way to show how much they revered the gods. They made it their mission to live a virtuous life as this would allow them to have a more tolerable existence in the afterlife, and serving the gods was part of this.

Some larger temples had storage rooms where treasures and other valuable offerings were stored for the deity to whom they had been offered.

Oracles were another way for the ancient Greeks to reach out to their gods. Even here, the deities couldn't be addressed directly, so a person would offer themselves to become the conductor of divine messages. This person was an oracle (usually a woman) who could temporarily stand on the threshold of the mortal world and the divine realm. Through an oracle, people learned what the gods intended for their lives, what they expected from them in the future, and what would happen if they obeyed or disobeyed what was expected of them. The oracles worked at religious sites where they could make a connection to the gods or goddesses' essences. Some of the most famous Oracle sites were the Oracle of Zeus at Dodona and the Oracle of Apollo at Delphi. At the latter resided Pythia, a popular oracle who communicated with Apollo, the god of prophecy, healing, light, and music. The Oracle of Delhi is also one of the oldest in existence, built in Apollo's honor when he slayed Python, the monster sent by Hera to torment his mother.

Sanctuaries also had gathering places for people to meet as many did not only come for the ritual but to be part of the community and share their common cultural and mythical heritage. For example, the sanctuaries of Aphrodite had places for picnics as well. Sometimes, these gathering places were infrequently used. By contrast, during annual celebrations, where everyone from the city (and beyond) participated, they were filled to the brim.

How the Greeks Honored Their Deities in Daily Life

The gods and goddesses influenced every aspect of life in ancient Greece, from daily actions through art and architecture to warfare. Moreover, time-honored traditions permeated personal life and were not just observed during formal rituals at sacred places. The ancient Greeks had a slightly different relationship with their gods than the followers of modern religions. Because they believed that the deities could influence mortal life and that they would always welcome acts of worship, they did everything they could to appease the gods in their daily lives. More than that, they thought that serving the gods was one of their major roles in life.

If not, the gods could decide that the mortals behaved awfully and must be punished or, worse, destroyed, which, according to the myths, had happened several times throughout history.

So, how did they make sure their gods and goddesses stayed happy? They found a way to include them in small actions. For example, they considered drinking wine and strong spirits a way to honor Dionysus, the god of wine. They believed that every time they drank these beverages, they took in the god's essence, which pleased them. This is why drinking wine was an integral part of daily life in ancient Greece.

During harvest season, they made sure to pray and make offerings to Demeter, ensuring a great year. Passionate agriculturalists, the Greeks did not only live on grains, grapes, and olives but traded their home-grown products for other commodities. Being dedicated to the goddess of the harvest and fertility was their way of securing their living. In springtime, they prayed to and offered regular sacrifices to Persephone, who could make nature come to life when she returned from the underworld. This was the Greeks' ingenious way of explaining the changing seasons.

Hestia, the goddess of fire, was responsible for feeding the hearth at Mount Olympus, and the Greeks honored her by meticulously tending to the hearths at their own homes every day. They also tended to the fire at the prytaneum, the public space with a hearth in the center. Prytaneums acted as gathering locations and places to honor Hestia. The Greeks believed they would bring good fortune to the community, city and loved ones by honoring Hestia publicly and at home. If the flame went out, this was considered sacrilege. If it happened due to someone's negligence, the person would receive severe punishment. Hestia was also given an offering in private homes before dinner and the first and last offering at many communal feasts.

Ancient Greeks used fire to keep warm, cook, make weapons and crafts, and even sacrifice, so it is no wonder that they revered it — and not just because of Hestia. The gift of fire was given to people by Prometheus, who was brutally punished by Zeus for his actions, so he deserves to be honored as well. Besides prayers and sacrifices, the Greeks had other ways to worship Prometheus. For example, the potters of Athens, who couldn't have thrived without fire in their kilns, gave homage to Prometheus with a yearly Promethea torch race.

Fishermen, merchants thriving on the fish trade, and sailors revered Poseidon, the sea god who could grant them safe voyages and work across the seas. As ancient Greece was surrounded by seas, this meant that a lot of people put their lives and livelihoods in Poseidon's hands. They built cities in his honor and had annual musical and athletic competitions dedicated to him. They considered all this necessary because, according to the legends, Poseidon was easily angered. So, the larger the gift or offering in his honor was, the higher the chances were that he would be pleased. Poseidon was also associated with natural phenomena over or related to water. If there was an unexpected natural disaster like a storm or earthquake, the ancient Greeks would immediately pray and make offerings to Poseidon.

Gaea, the creator of the primordial parts of the universe, including her son Uranus, was another Greek divine being worshiped universally. According to some accounts, she may have had the same number of followers, if not more, across Greece as Zeus. Many Greeks also honored Gaea just as followers of modern religion honor the beings they believed created the universe.

They erected temples and made regular animal sacrifices in her honor. Gaea was also known for her prophetic powers, as many oracles claimed that they learned their craft from her and were inspired to pursue their future-seeking journeys through her teachings. They included the goddess in their prayers before their work and did the same when they had public readings and rituals.

Athena, the goddess of wisdom, justice, craft, and war and the advisor of many heroes, was another highly revered deity. Craftsmen and philosophers felt inspired by Athena, prompting them to make regular offerings to her. Intelligence and hand skills were both highly revered qualities, and, as it was believed they came from Athena, it was crucial to honor her properly.

Many temples were built in her honor, and of course, the city of Athens is named after her. Due to her friendship with heroes like Odysseus, Achilles, Hercules, and Perseus, Athena was the most relatable goddess. She was easy to please and fruitful in her blessings. Gifting an olive branch was a regular custom to honor Athena, as the goddess gave one to the Athenians when she wanted to win their patronage.

Traders and road builders found their own divine supporter in Hermes, another highly influential Greek god. He was also relatable because he wasn't perfect. His myths describe him as triumphing despite his flaws and mistakes, which made him very inspirational. So, besides those who undertook creating and using the new roads and trade routes, those who wished to find solutions to seemingly impossible problems also turned to him. Another reason Hermes was worshiped was because the Greeks believed he could convey a message to the gods. It was widely known that he connected mortals to divine beings because he could cross the divides between the Earth and Mount Olympus. Moreover, he was one of the few who could travel between Earth and the Underworld, so he could be asked to deliver messages to deceased loved ones.

Conclusion

To summarize everything you've learned, for the ancient Greeks, religion was a way of life. Their deities were numerous, and they all had powers to admire or to cower in fear from. To appease their gods and goddesses, the Greeks built temples and made regular sacrifices to them.

Besides ensuring that the deities would support them instead of destroying their followers, divine worship in ancient Greece also had other purposes. Many believed that the gods and goddesses could help mortals become divine beings themselves. Greek mythology is riddled with tales of mortal heroes who achieved divine status or were gifted powers after committing an extraordinary deed.

The divine beings were ascribed different powers, although they generally stayed in the same realm, ruling either the Earth, sea, or heaven. Myths took them on diverse adventures, depending on the period and location from which they originated.

To complicate matters, there was a complex relationship between the deities, both the main ones and the lesser beings. Punctuated with rivalries, conflicts, and disregard for anything but power, these relationships often affected people's lives — at least this is how the Greeks saw it happen.

Highly religious, the ancient Greeks explained everything that occurred in their lives with an act from a deity. Their surroundings, livelihood, and many aspects of day-to-day life were tied to religious myths. These were interwoven into folklore, rituals, and actions. Their stories were passed down through generations to ensure those to come would know how to stay alive by appeasing the gods.

The lesser deities and mythical beings, the nymphs, satyrs, and other nature spirits that inhabited the Greek landscape also affected people's lives because they could influence nature, even if their impact wasn't as great as that of the Olympians.

The ancient creation myth is another fascinating aspect of Greek mythology. It shows an unorganized space giving birth to Earth, which, paradoxically, became the most supervised (if one is to believe the myriad of roles of all divine beings) place that ever existed.

Then, with the birth of the Titans, began an era of supreme rule. This authority was transferred to the Olympians when they defeated the Titans. This is another tale of the intricate power struggle that took place in the Greek pantheon, one which solidified the Greeks' belief in the might of their gods and goddesses.

The stories of the ages of humanity are equally perplexing but nevertheless entertaining. These, along with regular worship and communication with the divine beings, laid the foundation of what became one of the most fruitful and thought-inspiring mythologies in history.

References

101.school. (2023). Ancient Greek 101 - 101.school. 101.School. https://101.school/courses/ancient-greek-101/modules/9-ancient-greek-mythology/units/3-the-role-of-mythology-in-ancient-society

123Helpme.com. (2024). Role Of Sacrifice In Ancient Greece - 859 Words | 123 Help Me. 123helpme.com. https://www.123helpme.com/essay/Role-Of-Sacrifice-In-Ancient-Greece-FCWNAJWCT

Aaron J. Atsma. (2000). PERSEPHONE - Greek Goddess of Spring, Queen of the Underworld (Roman Proserpina). Theoi.com. https://www.theoi.com/Khthonios/Persephone.html

Atsma, A. (2000). JUDGEMENT OF PARIS - Greek Mythology. Theoi.com. https://www.theoi.com/Olympios/JudgementParis.html

Cartwright, M. (2019, September 10). The 12 Olympian Gods. World History Encyclopedia. https://www.worldhistory.org/collection/58/the-12-olympian-gods/#google_vignette

Centre of Excellence. (2024, March 8). The Most Powerful Greek Demigods: Myths of Strength and Heroism - Centre of Excellence. Www.centreofexcellence.com. https://www.centreofexcellence.com/powerful-greek-demigods/

Gill, N. S. (2019, October 29). Five Ages of Man in Greek Mythology According to Hesiod. ThoughtCo. https://www.thoughtco.com/the-five-ages-of-man-111776

Greek Mythology. (n.d.). https://www.marsd.org/cms/lib7/NJ01000603/Centricity/Domain/761/Greek%20Mythology.pdf

GreekMythology.com. (2015, August 2). Narcissus - Greek Mythology. Greekmythology.com; GreekMythology.com. https://www.greekmythology.com/Myths/Mortals/Narcissus/narcissus.html

Hays, J. (n.d.). Ancient Greek Temples, Sanctuaries and Sacred Places | Early European History And Religion — Facts and Details. Europe.factsanddetails.com. https://europe.factsanddetails.com/article/entry-178.html

Herzog, M. (2023). Mount Olympus in Greek Mythology | Location & Importance. Study.com. https://study.com/academy/lesson/mount-olympus-in-greek-mythology.html

Hunt, J. M. (2019). Greek Mythology Gods Olympians. Desy.de. https://www.desy.de/gna/interpedia/greek_myth/olympian.html

Hunt, J. M. (2024). Greek Mythology Gods Titans. Desy.de. https://www.desy.de/gna/interpedia/greek_myth/titan.html#Titans

J. Atsma, A. (2017). SATYRS (Satyroi) - Fertility Spirits of Greek Mythology (Roman Fauns). Theoi.com. https://www.theoi.com/Georgikos/Satyroi.html

J. Atsma, A. (n.d.). NYMPHS (Nymphai) - Nature Spirits of Greek Mythology. Www.theoi.com. https://www.theoi.com/Nymphe/Nymphai.html

Macquire, K. (2022). World History Encyclopedia. Worldhistory.org. https://www.worldhistory.org/video/2855/oracles-of-ancient-greece

Madeleine. (2019, September 13). Top 10 Greek Heroes in Mythology -. Theoi. https://www.theoi.com/articles/top-10-greek-heroes-in-mythology/

Madeleine. (2019, September 13). What Is the Greek Creation Myth? -. Theoi. https://www.theoi.com/articles/what-is-the-greek-creation-myth/

Ms Mcclure. (2015). Introduction to-greek-mythology-powerpoint. SlideShare; Slideshare. https://www.slideshare.net/slideshow/introduction-togreekmythologypowerpoint/55634337

Murtagh, L. (2019). Creation Myths -- Greek Creation Myth. Williams.edu. https://www.cs.williams.edu/~lindsey/myths/myths_16.html

My Learning. (2019). Greek Mythology and Gods • Ancient Greeks: Everyday Life, Beliefs and Myths • MyLearning. Mylearning.org. https://www.mylearning.org/stories/ancient-greeks-everyday-life-beliefs-and-myths/415

Nikos. (n.d.). GreekMythologyTours - The 12 Olympian Gods and Goddesses of Ancient Greece. Greekmythologytours.com. https://greekmythologytours.com/blog/greek-mythology/12-olympian-gods

The J. Paul Getty Museum. (n.d.). Aphrodite and the Gods of Love: Mythology (Getty Villa Exhibitions). Www.getty.edu. https://www.getty.edu/art/exhibitions/aphrodite/myth.html